DISCARD

SO-BJM-902

ARTIFICIAL HUMANS

Transplants
and
Bionics

ARTIFICIAL

Transplants
and
Bionics

HUMANS

Thomas H. Metos

Illustrated with photographs

Julian Messner  New York

Published by Julian Messner,
A Division of Simon & Schuster, Inc.
Simon & Schuster Building,
1230 Avenue of the Americas,
New York, New York 10020.
JULIAN MESSNER and colophon are trademarks of
Simon & Schuster, Inc.

Manufactured in the United States of America

Design by Teresa Delgado, A Good Thing, Inc.

Library of Congress Cataloging in Publication Data

Metos, Thomas H.
  Artificial humans.

  Includes index.
  Summary: Describes how transplants can save lives
and how they have improved over the years. Also
discusses continuing research on how to produce better
functioning artificial parts.
  1. Artificial organs—Juvenile literature.
2. Prosthesis—Juvenile literature. [1. Artificial
organs. 2. Prosthesis] I. Title.
RD130.M48 1985   617'.95   84-22818
ISBN 0-671-44367-4

To My Family
and
Mady

MESSNER BOOKS BY THOMAS H. METOS

Artificial Humans
Robots A₂Z

With Gary G. Bitter
Exploring With Solar Energy

PHOTO CREDITS

Intermedics Corp., pp. 21, 23, 24, 26, 49, 54, 55, 56, 57, 59, 60, 71, 72, 83

University of Utah Medical Center, pp. 13, 18, 43, 46, 47, 62–3, 65, 67, 73, 74, 77, 78

University of Utah *Review*, p. 12

ACKNOWLEDGMENTS

Grateful acknowledgment is made to the individuals and institutions who made this book possible:

Olga van Dura of the Division of Artificial Organs at the University of Utah; S. Byron Sims of the University of Utah *Review*; Ted Swift of Intermedics Inc.; and the University of Arizona Medical Center.

For their help and advice, special recognition is given to Clinton R. Burt and Jeffery Metos.

Finally, without the special skills of Carol Hansen and Lois Kinkaid, this book would not have been completed. Thank you.

CONTENTS

INTRODUCTION

In *The Empire Strikes Back*, Luke Skywalker fights with Darth Vader and has his hand cut off by a laser sword. Later in the movie, we find Luke alive, fitted with an artificial hand that looks and acts like his original hand. Although this movie and TV shows like "The Bionic Woman" and "The Six Million Dollar Man" with their super-powered heroine and hero don't show real situations, they *are* based on present-day scientific research.

Scientists, engineers, doctors, and technicians are working in laboratories, universities, and hospitals throughout the world to develop devices that will replace diseased or damaged human organs or limbs. Some of these artificial parts have been used for a long time and have saved many lives. Some, like the artificial heart, are brand new.

In December 1982, news was broadcast around the world of the first permanent implant of an artificial heart in a human patient. Barney Clark, a 61-year-old retired dentist who was dying from heart disease, had an aluminum and plastic pump implanted in his chest

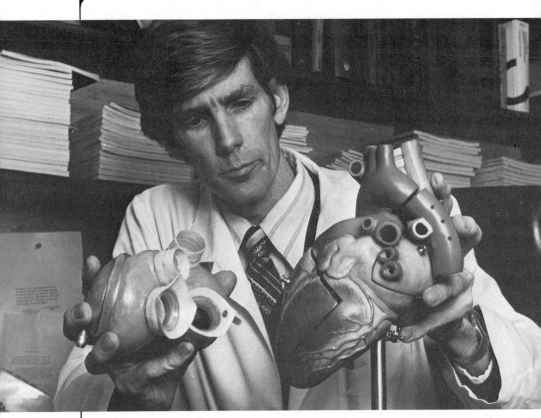

Dr. William DeVries, the surgeon who replaced Barney Clark's heart, compares the Jarvik-7 artificial heart (left) with an instructional model of a natural heart.

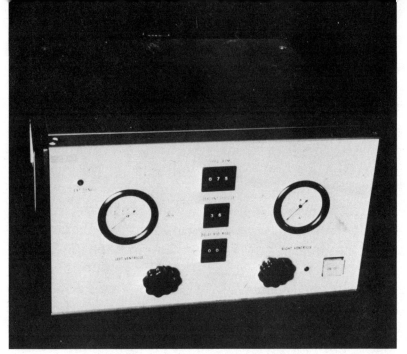

The air pump that powered Barney Clark's artificial heart.

to replace his damaged heart. Clark's artificial heart was powered by a 365-pound air pump machine connected to his body by two six-foot hoses. After two operations to correct mechanical difficulties in his new heart, Clark was well enough to move around the hospital with his air pump machine following him. But after 112 days, Barney Clark died. His new heart had not stopped; the rest of his body had died.

There are many problems with organ replacement, whether with an artificial organ like Dr. Clark's heart or with a transplant of a living organ. Transplants of living organs are not always available. In 1984, doctors tried to solve this problem by transplanting a baboon heart into a baby whose own heart had failed. Baby Fae lived for a short while, but the many problems of such a transplant finally resulted in death. Transplants are often rejected by the body because they are foreign to it. Or drugs used to help the body accept the organ may cause other serious problems. Artificial organs ordinarily do not have problems of rejection by the body, but not all organs can be duplicated as yet. And many of those that have been duplicated have a long way to go to function perfectly.

Scientists are working hard toward producing better functioning artificial parts for humans: kidneys, eyes, ears, joints, limbs, skin, blood, and other organs, including the brain. This engineering of parts to perform human functions is called *bionics* or *biomedical engineering*.

⚜ Artificial Limbs

A *prosthesis*—artificial part—is usually thought of as an artificial arm or leg. But, in fact, the word also refers to replacements for bones, arteries, heart valves, eyes, and teeth. Even eyeglasses and hearing aids are classified as prostheses.

Prostheses—more than one prosthesis—for human beings can be traced back to almost the beginning of the human race. Crutches, canes, and walking sticks or staffs were used to aid human beings who were deformed or who had lost a limb through accident.

The history of *prosthetics*—the science of designing and making prostheses—goes back to the 1500s and the French surgeon Ambroise Paré. Paré was a pioneer in many surgical techniques, especially for those wounded in war. He was the first to tie off arteries instead of using boiling oil to stop bleeding. He is given credit for being the first doctor to fit artificial limbs to amputees. The limbs were crude devices of metal and wood, but they helped. Other surgeons in other countries followed Paré's lead. History tells of a German knight who lost his arm in battle and was fitted with an artificial arm that had levers and gears that actually moved his jointed fingers. His career as a warrior was continued and, in fact, the Knight of the Iron Hand was more dangerous than ever.

By the 1700s, the solid hand gave way to the metal hook or a leather-covered imitation hand attached by a wooden or leather shell and leather straps.

It was not until the twentieth century, during World Wars I and II, that any real progress was made in the design of artificial limbs. Newer and lighter materials—such as fiberglass–reinforced plastics— were used, and improvements were made in mechanical joints, so the limbs were more flexible. They were more comfortable to wear as well as more usable. But straps, belts, and corsets that attached the limbs remained bulky, heavy, and annoying.

After World War II, two advances in prosthetics made artificial arms much more attractive. The use of strong and lightweight materials made it possible to attach the arm to the shoulder with webbing. A steel cable ran from the webbing to the end of the arm, ending either in a steel hook or a mechanical hand. Shrugging one's shoulders activated the steel cable to either open or close the hook, enabling one to pick up, grasp, and hold objects. This made the artificial arm a useful tool, not something just for appearance's sake. But it was difficult to use and didn't accomplish enough for the effort, so many people stopped using it.

The mechanical hand developed after World War II by the U.S. Army was better than the cable-powered hook. The mechanical hand, covered with rubber to look as realistic as possible, was operated by battery-powered electrical energy. The hand was activated by wires attached to electrodes in the wearer's arm muscles. By contracting or relaxing certain muscles in the arm, the hand was activated to grasp, pick up, and hold objects. All five fingers of the hand could be manipulated separately as well.

Today, many of the newer artificial limbs are attached to the leg or arm through the use of a suction device. They need no straps or harnesses.

Recently, the University of Utah announced the availability of a new artificial arm called the "Utah Arm." The arm is rugged, light, and uses small electric motors powered by batteries. It is made to move by sensory electrodes implanted in the skin. Just thinking about the movement will make the limb move. Made especially for those people whose arms have been severed above the elbow, it takes less energy to operate and is less bulky in appearance than those that used

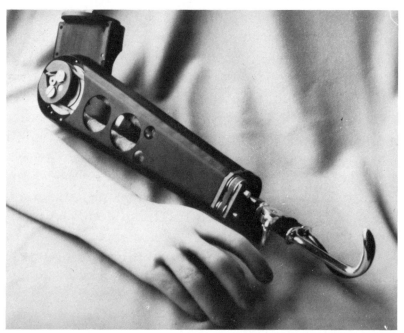

The Utah Artificial Arm.

cables. Electrodes implanted in the skin of the shoulder monitor impulses and cause the arm to move just as our brains monitor impulses and transmit them to our muscles to make them move.

The complicated motions of the hand are still being worked on to achieve a powered hand that will be able to act in most ways as a normal hand does. Eventually, electrodes will be attached to nerves so that just thinking of a motion will cause that motion, not only in arms but also in hands and legs.

Artificial parts for human beings can also be used for animals. In 1982, at the Seattle Zoo, a baby Simian ape was fitted with an artificial arm to replace the one chewed off by its father. Because apes get around by swinging, an ape without an arm is severely handicapped. Fitted with an artificial arm by a local surgeon, the young Simian now happily swings around with the other apes.

Artificial Joints

The 1940s and 1950s saw the development of artificial *joints*—the connecting point of two or more bones —made of artificial bone and connecting materials. Much of this work was done because of the large number of wounded soldiers from World War II and the

Korean conflict who needed artificial limbs and joints. The materials used are called *biomaterials* and the field of specialization, *biomechanics*. Professor Carl Hirsch of Sweden is one of the most renowned of biomechanics. He used engineering instruments to calculate the stress and strain on joints and bones and applied that knowledge to the development of artificial implants that would take these stresses and strains. Examples of such implants are artificial teeth, bones, hip sockets, and finger joints.

The human body will normally reject foreign objects implanted in the body or cause many of these artificial parts to corrode. Blood contains many organic acids that start to dissolve the parts and thus weakens them. Some metals, needed for strength, were either poisonous, too easily corroded, or broke easily. This was true of steel. However, certain metals were light, strong, hard, durable, and could be highly polished or plated to make a smooth surface for ease of movement. Vitallium was a good metal to use, but it had to be cast. Later, a better metal, 18/12 (a combination of stainless steel, chrome, nickel, and other elements) proved more effective. Still later, titanium was found to be useful. Today, platinum, gold, iridium, aluminum, cobalt, nickel,

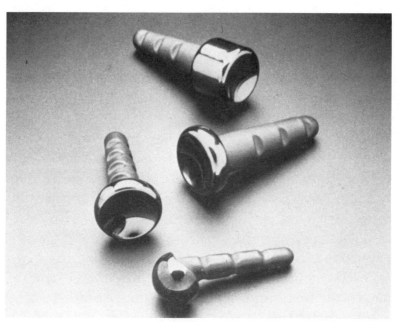

Pyrolite carbon artificial finger joints.

chromium, and molybdenum—individually or in combination—are in use. Manufactured artificial substances such as polyethylene plastic, alumina, bioglass, silicone, dacron, and carbon fibers are used for joint and bone parts.

In 1963, an English surgeon, John Charnley, performed the first total hip replacement operation. The hip joint is made up of the *femur*—thigh bone—which rotates in a socket or depression in the *pelvis*—the bone that runs across the bottom of the abdomen. The hip is easily broken or attacked by arthritis. Dr. Charnley used a metal ball to replace the top of the femur. A cup-shaped plastic device was cemented to the pelvis bone to act as the socket for the top of the femur. The hip joint had to move with the least amount of friction possible and the cup-shaped socket device had to stay firmly in the pelvis so that movement would not twist it from the bone. A cement—methyl methacrylate—was found to be tremendously strong, and when setting or drying, it did not generate heat, which could destroy the bone. This is the standard way of cementing bones and joint replacements today.

Following Charnley's successful hip replacement operation, Michigan scientists developed a successful knee-joint replacement. It eliminated the abrupt stop of earlier devices that made knee replacement unpractical. The patient would fall, or the joint would be wrenched loose by the force of the stop.

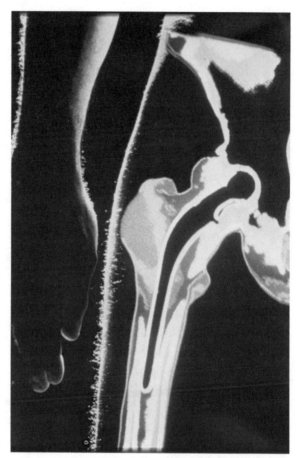

An artificial implanted hip device.

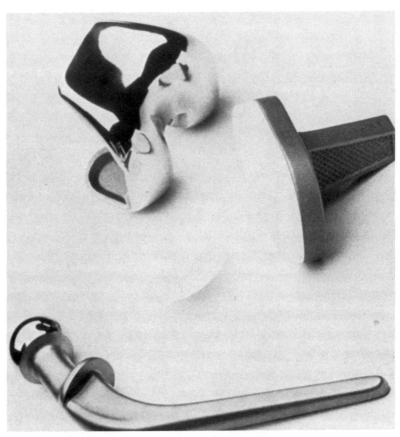

Close-up of an artificial hip device.

Today there are almost daily announcements of new discoveries and applications of artificial parts for the body. Three of the most recent developments are of artificial *bone, tendons*—the attachment tissues of muscles to bones—and *ligaments*—the thin muscle attachments holding joints and organs in place.

☃ Artificial Bone

Metal screws and pins can hold or join damaged bone until it can regenerate itself. However, there are times when bone cannot regenerate quickly enough, and artificial bone is needed. Battelle Columbus Laboratory of Ohio has done a great deal of work with artificial bone.

The artificial bone developed by Battelle is *biodegradable*—it will dissolve over a period of time. The artificial bone is made of TCP, a ceramic or china-like substance. TCP can be used as a powder or granules, or can be formed into sheets. Not strong enough for use in long bones, the artificial bone is soft enough to carve with a knife and can be shaped or

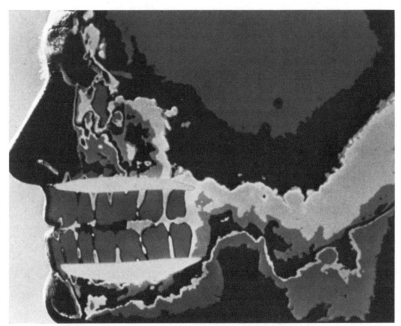
Artificial bone used for dental and orthopedic surgery.

formed for skull or jaw repairs. TCP is porous, allowing the cells from surrounding bone tissue to enter and form new bone. After one or two years, the biodegradable ceramic dissolves, leaving freshly formed bone in its place.

Tendons and Ligaments

In 1981, the U.S. Food and Drug Administration approved the trial use of artificial tendons and ligaments. Tendons and ligaments tear in falls or during violent exertions of athletes. They take a long time to heal. Artificial tendons and ligaments, developed by researchers in New Jersey, are made up of approximately ten thousand fine carbon filaments, each a six-millionth of a meter in diameter, with a plastic coating.

Surgeons arrange the fibers of the artificial tendons or ligaments to replace the damaged ones. The artificial tendons or ligaments are not for permanent placement. They act as a temporary, biodegradable ladder or connecting rod from muscle to bone. *Fibroblasts*—blood cells that form tough, fibrous tissue—attach themselves to the artificial fibers and form connective tissue. At the same time, *collagen*—scar tissue—is forming. By the time the carbon fibers and plastic coating are dissolved by the body, new connecting and scar tissue is in their place. Although still too early to tell for sure, reports indicate that the artificial materials work quite successfully, especially in repairing knee, heel, and ankle tendons and ligaments.

Plastic Surgery

Plastic surgeons for many years have operated on patients who wish to improve their appearance by reshaping unattractive features or smoothing away the signs of age. Other patients need the services of plastic surgeons to repair their appearance because of accident, surgery, birth defect, or disease.

A new advance in plastic surgery is the use of Zyderm, a collagen substance obtained from cattle.

Collagen, suspended in a liquid, is presently being used to replace flesh behind depressed scars without resorting to actual surgery. The Zyderm is injected under the scar with a hypodermic needle until the scar is raised. Natural collagen eventually replaces the injected Zyderm, which slowly dissolves. This procedure is especially useful for skin cancer patients who have deep scars where the cancer is surgically removed.

The plastic surgeon works with stainless steel and other metal screws, plates and wires, bioglass, artificial bone, artificial skin, silicone Teflon sponge, silicone rubber, collagen fluid, Dacron fabric, acrylic resin, graphite fibers, and many other biomaterials. The surgeon may also turn to such prosthetic devices as artificial ears, fingers, toes, feet, breasts, eyes, and even portions of the head and face.

For the most part, these prosthetic devices are cosmetic in nature. Occasionally, though, they may be designed to function like the real part of the body. A hand might actually move or grasp objects. Cosmetic parts are made of silicone and are soft and pliable like real flesh and skin. The parts are finished to show hair, wrinkles, freckles, and veins, in contrast to artificial devices that are usually just hard plastic shells and do not look lifelike at all.

Many cosmetic parts are made by dental technicians who are already experienced in making artificial parts like teeth, bridges, and prosthetic devices for the mouth. Horst Buckner, a former dental technician, was recently featured in newspapers around the country as one of the leading makers of cosmetic artificial human parts. Besides making facial parts, Buckner makes hands, toes, fingers, and breasts. These parts are extremely lifelike, and before being attached, Buckner tries to match them as closely to the patient's skin tone and texture as possible.

One of Buckner's recent accomplishments was the building of an artificial foot for a twenty-five-year-old woman who had lost all but the heel of her foot in an accident at age twelve. He reproduced a foot out of silicone, using the woman's real foot as a model. Buckner then painted the artificial foot, right down to the toenails. The artificial foot is slipped on like a sock and is held to the ankle by medical glue. The woman is no longer self-conscious about showing her foot in shoes or without them. The foot is also functional. Although the woman could walk on her heel alone, her new foot felt good, and better protected her leg against the impact of walking.

𝕊 Artificial Blood

Our blood, pumped by the heart, moves continuously through the body. Carried by the veins, blood enters the right side of the heart and then is carried to the lungs to pick up oxygen. It then moves back to the left side of the heart where it is pumped out to the body through the vast network of arteries and capillaries. The blood carries the life-giving oxygen to all the cells of the body and picks up carbon dioxide and other wastes for disposal, then starts the cycle again to the left side of the heart.

For every 2.2 pounds (1 kg) of body weight we have about 2.3 ounces (70 milliliters) of blood. Therefore, a person weighing 180 pounds (81.8 kg) has nearly six quarts of blood in his or her body. Though it looks like a liquid, blood is really a body tissue. The cells are not joined together as in other body tissue but are suspended in the fluid portion of the blood, called *plasma*. Approximately fifty-five percent of blood is plasma. The other forty-five percent is made up of red blood cells, white blood cells, and cells called platelets.

Blood carries oxygen to the body cells and removes

wastes. Blood also regulates our internal environment, that is, it keeps our bodies from becoming too hot or cold. The blood does this by absorbing heat from the body's internal organs and then releasing that heat when it passes near the skin's surface. The blood is also vital in protecting us from infection. Certain cells in the blood attack and kill bacteria, while others produce antibodies, a special protein. Antibodies respond to foreign bacteria and viruses to make them ineffective.

Early human beings believed that blood had certain mystical qualities. Some groups held ritual ceremonies with blood, and many worshipped it. They knew that blood was the vital fluid of the body but didn't really know how it functioned. As late as 1492, physicians gave the mortally ill Pope Innocent VII the blood of three young men to drink. The young men lost their lives in the process, and the pope's life was not saved.

In the early seventeenth century, after William Harvey discovered how the circulatory system worked, it was thought that some sick people could be cured through injections of human or animal blood. Most of these experiments ended in disaster, because no one knew then that there were different types of blood that could not mix.

It was not until 1901 that the differences in blood were discovered. Austrian Karl Fondsteiner found that human blood was divided into four different types—A, B, AB, and O. In the United States, forty-five percent of the population have type O, forty-one percent have type A, ten percent have type B, and four percent have type AB. Because of certain substances or lack of them in each type of blood, it was discovered that type O blood could be transfused to any person, regardless of type of blood, and that individuals with type AB blood could receive transfusions of any other blood type. Thus, type O individuals are known as universal donors and type AB individuals as universal recipients.

In 1940, a second major difference in blood types was made. This was of the *Rh factor.* "Rh" comes from Rhesus, as this research was carried out on Rhesus monkeys. It was found that there were two Rh factors, Rh positive (Rh+) or Rh negative (Rh−).

There is great danger in blood transfusions involving different Rh types. In some pregnancies, there can be an incompatibility between a mother's and baby's blood. Harmful and often fatal reactions to these blood differences occur unless the newborn child's blood is replaced.

Today we know of at least eighty different substances in the blood that affect its compatibility for transfusions.

In addition to the problems of matching blood types, there is the problem of availability. Human blood can come from several major sources. One, of course, is from the donor directly to the patient. Another is from blood banks in which whole blood is stored. A source used widely in the Soviet Union, but not elsewhere, is blood from *cadavers*—dead bodies. When blood cannot be readily matched, on the battlefield or in emergencies, plasma is used. Plasma doesn't have to be matched to the patient's blood, but plasma is not as restorative as whole blood.

Still another danger in blood transfusions is that of disease. Blood from a diseased donor can sometimes affect the recipient. Diseases that can be easily transmitted by blood are jaundice and hepatitis, diseases of the liver, and AIDS—acquired immune deficiency syndrome. Jaundice can be transmitted years after the donor has had the disease and can kill the person receiving the blood.

For all of these reasons, researchers have been working on the development and practical use of artificial blood. The researchers have been looking for a fluid that is inexpensive, usable by all, easily available, and safe, with no side effects. Such fluids are being developed. Most researchers are using fluorocarbons. However, others are investigating the use of chemically-sterilized *hemoglobin*—colored protein blood cells—from waste blood. One Japanese firm, Green Cross Corporation, has developed an artificial blood it plans to market commercially very soon. The Japanese company calls its product Fluosol-DA. Fluosol is primarily made of perfluorodecalin, a fluorine and carbon substance like the materials used on non-stock frying pans.

Fluosol-DA has been tried successfully on animals and over three hundred human patients in Japan. In the United States, several people have received the artificial blood.

Fluosol-DA, though only a temporary blood substitute, does have some remarkable qualities. It can be stored frozen for a much longer time than human blood, which has a storage life of only about thirty-five days. Fluosol does not carry diseases, and it is compatible with all other types of blood. It can pass more easily than real blood through diseased or clogged veins or arteries as its particles are smaller—only one-seventieth the size of blood cells. Fluosol-DA also has an extraordinary capacity to carry large amounts of oxygen throughout the body. In fact, in one experiment, small animals were submerged in water and injected with Fluosol-DA and had enough oxygen in their bodies to prevent them from drowning.

However, Fluosol-DA lasts only about thirty-six hours in the body. It evaporates through the skin and is exhaled. Also, Fluosol cannot fight disease as the real blood does. At present, Fluosol is used solely for emergencies. Scientists believe, however, that Fluosol or similar substances will be important in countries with high incidences of blood diseases or for uses other than blood transfusion. For example, Fluosol-DA, with its great ability to carry high amounts of oxygen, may be used to revive victims of carbon monoxide poisoning, or to preserve donor organs, or to transmit large amounts of oxygen to heart and stroke victims.

Besides the Japanese, there are others who are attempting to develop blood substitutes. For example, the U.S. Army is trying to develop a blood substitute from chemically-altered blood. The Army's artificial blood, like Fluosol, can be transfused to anyone, but it must be mixed with whole blood; so the matching problem is still unsolved. It carries large amounts of oxygen and may be very effective in treating heart attack and stroke victims. However, the substance has no clotting properties, so it can leak out in an accident. The Army has tested with no harmful results its artificial blood on animals and soon plans to start tests on humans.

Artificial Skin

Artificial skin is another recent discovery, one that promises life to thousands of burn victims. Our skin is the largest organ of our body. The skin on an adult can weigh as much as ten pounds and cover up to 18.5 square feet. Skin fulfills a number of vital functions. The skin protects us from the elements, helps regulate our body temperature, provides us with sensations, and keeps us from losing vital blood and water.

Many people who are badly burned die because they lack skin to hold body fluids in or keep bacterial infection out. Doctors treat the patient by graftng skin from an unburned part of the body to cover the burned part, or if this is not possible, by using skin from pigs or from people who recently have died. But foreign skin is rejected by the body in three to twenty-five days, often not long enough for the patient to survive.

In 1981, John Burre, a surgeon from Boston, and Ioannis Yannas, a professor of engineering at the Massachusetts Institute of Technology, announced their discovery of artificial skin. Its use on ten patients showed no rejection of the artificial skin nor any resulting infection. The artificial skin consists of two layers. The inner layer is made up of cowhide and shark cartilage that have been mixed together in an acid solution and changed into fibers. These short, white fibers are then frozen, dried, placed in a vacuum to remove moisture, then baked into a sheet. This inner sheet is bonded to the top or outer layer, a sticky plastic. The artificial skin is then freeze-dried and stored in sterile containers to await use.

Artificial skin is soft and flexible, much like the human skin. It is draped on the burned areas in patches as large as six by ten inches. The artificial skin allows the nerves and blood vessels to grow into it so normal sensations can be felt.

The artificial skin isn't a perfect replacement but seems to protect the burned area until real skin can be grafted or grown onto the area. Scientists who are working on artificial skin are aiming for a permanent skin covering, so that further grafts will no longer be necessary.

🜚 Kidneys

The development of artificial organs has captured the most attention in newspapers, radio, and on TV. Stories of artificial kidneys, hearts, livers, eyes, and ears are meant to attract readers and viewers and so are often exaggerated. But the reality can be more fascinating than the fiction.

The kidney is one of the few organs that we have in duplicate. The kidneys are a pair of organs that are located on either side of the spine on the back wall of the abdominal cavity. Each kidney is about 4½ inches long, two to three inches wide, one inch thick, and brownish in color. The kidney is covered by two layers of tissue to attach it to the body and protect it from injury. The main purpose of our kidneys is to cleanse the blood of waste substances by forming urine, which is then eliminated from the body.

Kidneys produce urine constantly. Depending on what a person eats and drinks, the kidneys produce anywhere from twenty to forty-eight ounces of urine daily. The kidney is also important in the formation of red blood cells and in stimulating certain glands to produce steroids. *Steroids* are compounds in the body that help to regulate such things as body growth, appetite, and digestion. Kidneys also help control blood pressure and break down food for body use—the *metabolic process.*

The kidney can be damaged by cancer, infections, diseases such as diabetes and high blood pressure, poisons, accidents, and birth defects. We can live with only one kidney, though. If one kidney is removed for any reason, we can easily survive on the remaining one if it is healthy. In fact, the remaining kidney will grow larger to work better. But if both kidneys fail, death is the result—unless a transplant or an artificial kidney can be used.

Over 30,000 individuals are alive today because of the invention of the artificial kidney. The cost of artificial kidneys is over 1.3 *billion* dollars per year.

An artificial kidney was worked on as far back as 1913, but it was not until 1943 that the first patient was hooked up to an artificial kidney to receive *dialysis*— separating poisonous waste urea from blood cells by a membrane that acts as a screen. Dr. Willem J. Kolff built this first artificial kidney.

Dr. Kolff, who practiced in the Netherlands, first became interested in developing an artificial kidney to separate impurities from blood and return the cleansed blood to the patient when one of his patients died of kidney disease. Shortly after, Dr. Kolff learned, as he puts it, of "the wonders of cellophane." Cellophane is a transparent paper-like substance used for wrappings, and Dr. Kolff hit on its use as a membrane for dialysis. Suspended in a special solution, the cellophane allowed urea but not the larger blood cells to pass through.

Dr. Kolff's first experiments were to determine how much cellophane would be needed to remove a certain amount of urea from a certain amount of blood and in how long a time. In the midst of his experiments, the German army invaded and then conquered the Netherlands. At first, Dr. Kolff was kept from his experiments. To help casualties of bombing, Dr. Kolff set up the first blood bank on the continent of Europe. This, as Dr. Kolff said, "gave him confidence in handling blood outside the body, and this is exactly what one does with an artificial kidney."

Dr. Kolff eventually continued his work on the artificial kidney, but because of the German occupation, he faced many problems. The Germans would not allow goods to be manufactured except for themselves. But the doctor persuaded a local factory to make certain parts he needed. He was never charged for the parts; the transactions could not appear on the records of the manufacturer.

The first artificial kidney was made of over sixty feet of cellophane tubing inside a drum. Blood taken from the patient entered the cellophane tubing. The drum, half-filled with dialysis fluid, then revolved slowly. The blood and dialysis fluid were constantly propelled by gravity to the lowest part of the drum. Here, the solution drew the urea out of the cellophane tubing.

The first drums were made of aluminum, but later had to be made of wooden laths because of the shortage

The first rotating artificial kidney—developed by Dr. Kolff.

created by the war. To eliminate leakage around the couplings of the laths, Dr. Kolff used packing borrowed from Ford automobile pumps.

On March 17, 1943, the first patient was treated with Dr. Kolff's artificial kidney. The patient was a twenty-nine-year-old woman suffering from kidney failure and several other medical problems that accompany kidney failure. She received twelve dialysis treatments. At first, the blood was drawn from the patient in a small amount, placed in the artificial kidney for dialysis, and then re-injected into the patient to see if any serious reactions would take place. When no serious reactions occurred, larger and larger amounts of blood were dialyzed, until almost six quarts of blood were being dialyzed. During the last treatments, the blood was continuously fed into, and returned from, the artificial kidney by tube.

Later, a pump was used to circulate the blood from patient to machine and back again. Then a permanent connection made of glass was inserted into one of the patient's arteries for the transfer of the blood.

For the next sixteen months, fifteen patients were treated with the artificial kidneys. Only one survived. Dr. Kolff was never sure whether the artificial kidney or his other medical treatment saved that patient's life.

As the war went on, Dr. Kolff continued his research on the artificial kidney. He built other machines and experimented with the dialysis fluid and drugs like *heparin,* used to thin the blood and to stop it from coagulating. At the end of the war, eight machines had been built—four were kept by the Dutch and four were given to other countries.

In 1950, Dr. Kolff left the Netherlands for a job in Cleveland, Ohio. In the United States, he developed an artificial kidney based on his machines built in the Netherlands. But his new model was much smaller—a juice can with cellophane wrapped around it. This was the basis for the simple, disposable artificial kidney found throughout the world today, although there are several other types of artificial kidneys available.

Most kidney patients have to go to a dialysis center for about twelve hours of treatment a week. This process is very expensive. Worse yet, the patient is tied to the machine for life. Researchers, including Dr. Kolff, are aiming toward portable and cheaper machines that will free the patient to live a more normal life.

In 1983, Gary Coleman, the young television star of "Different Strokes" and other shows, was fitted with an artificial kidney in his abdomen. Gary's earlier kidney transplant had failed, therefore he was in need of dialysis to live. Fitted with a dialysis bag and a tube into the wall of his abdomen, the membrane in the walls acting as a filter, Gary was able to lead an almost normal life until he received another kidney transplant in 1984.

A patient with a Wearable Artificial Kidney (WAK).

Wearable artificial kidneys, which are really portable dialysis machines, and artificial kidneys that use filters of charcoal or other substances to remove the toxic wastes of the blood, are being developed. So far, they can be used for only short periods of time. However, as

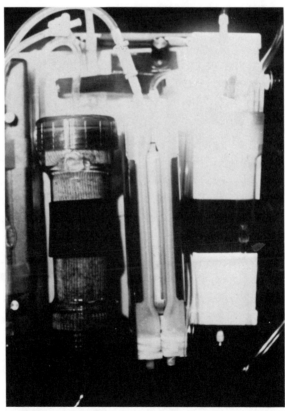

A close-up view of the Wearable Artificial Kidney.

research continues, it may not be too far in the future that a cheap, portable, and convenient artificial kidney may be available that would allow patients to live full and normal lives.

ॐ The Liver

One of the vital functions of the liver is to *detoxify,* or remove toxins and harmful substances from the blood. A damaged liver cannot remove toxins, and death results. An artificial liver is the object of much scientific research, which, to now, has been unsuccessful. So far the closest that surgeons have come to success is a surgically implanted pump intended to deliver cancer-fighting drugs to patients with liver cancer.

The pump weighs about a pound and is made of silicone rubber and metal. Implanted under the skin of the abdomen, the pump is connected to the artery that feeds blood to the liver. The pump then allows very high doses of drugs, one hundred to four hundred times greater than normal, to be fed directly into the cancerous liver. There are no dangerous side effects of nausea

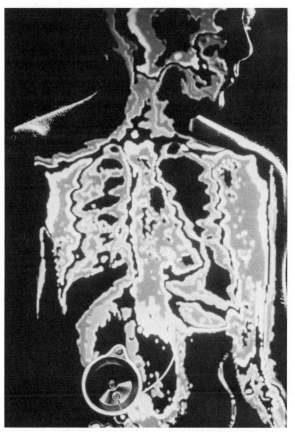

An implantable drug delivery system.

and loss of white blood cells such as those caused by radiation and the usual chemotherapy.

The pump does not cure the liver of cancer, but it does reduce the size of the cancer and extends the life span of the patient.

The Pancreas

Another organ that researchers have tried unsuccessfully to duplicate artificially is the pancreas. The pancreas is a very important gland situated close to the stomach. It makes and sends digestive juices to the stomach and produces the hormone insulin, which controls the level of sugar in the body. When the pancreas does not produce enough insulin, sugar in the body increases and causes the disease *diabetes*.

Injections of insulin are used to control the ups and downs of sugar levels in the body, but dosages are hard to adjust. Uncontrolled diabetes can cause blindness, heart and kidney damage, and circulatory problems that may end in amputation of limbs. Researchers decided that until an artificial pancreas was possible, a better way was needed to deliver insulin to the body than injections.

Several research groups have developed artificial insulin pumps that continually supply the body with insulin. Most of the insulin pumps in use today are battery-powered devices worn on a belt or in a shoulder holster. A small tube carries the insulin from the pump to a needle implanted under the skin. Every few minutes a drop of insulin is pumped automatically into the body. Some pumps are now controlled by silicon chips, the same chips that are used in pocket calculators and computers.

Scientists at the University of New Mexico Medical Center have announced that they have developed an insulin pump that is implanted in the body. Inserted into one side of the patient's abdomen is an eleven-ounce metal-encased package consisting of the pump, lithium batteries, and electronic controls. On the other side of the abdomen, connected to the pump, is a silicone rubber reservoir containing the insulin. The insulin reservoir is refilled every two days by a hypodermic needle. By using a control box (like a remote control for a television set), a patient can signal the pump to increase the flow of insulin to the body when needed, such as right after eating. This device is very close to being an artificial pancreas. While it has been used successfully in a human being, it is still in the experimental stage.

🎗 Artificial Heart

Of all the research and development done on artificial parts for humans, the artificial heart has captured the public's attention and received the most publicity. One of the major reasons for this high interest is that heart disease is the number one cause of death and disability in the United States. Every year over 500,000 people die in this country from heart attacks. Medical care in the United States for heart attack victims costs over $25 billion a year.

Human heart transplants have been performed since

1967. Of course, there are problems with transplants. One problem is the limited number of human hearts available for transplant. Another is the very powerful drugs which are used on the patient to prevent organ rejection. These drugs can cause severe problems for the patient. Therefore, Barney Clark's successful artificial heart caused great excitement. The search for an improved artificial heart continues. Today there are several types of artificial hearts ready for human experimentation.

Since the early 1800s, the notion that a human heart might be replaced with an artificial one has been the basis for many experiments. By 1920, a combined heart-lung machine was being investigated, based on an artificial lung developed by two Germans in 1855. By the 1950s, a successful heart-lung machine was introduced that allowed the stopping of the patient's heart and lungs during surgery.

The force behind the development of an artificial heart comes from the development of the heart-lung bypass machine. This machine takes over the body functions of pumping and oxygenating blood. By using the machine, surgeons are able to stop the heart to make surgical repairs or to allow a damaged heart to rest and recuperate. Surgeons are able to replace damaged parts of the heart with artificial parts. To properly regulate blood flow to and from the heart, artificial heart valves and artery replacements are becoming quite common. Sometimes the heart valves are replaced with a material made from carbon. Dacron

Mechanical heart valves.

Pyrolite carbon heart valve parts are polished to a micro finish for smoother blood flow.

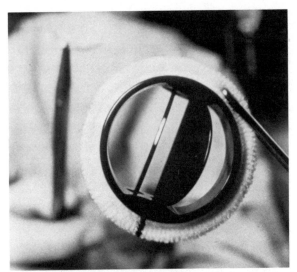

Mechanical heart valve is readied for the surgical team.

pieces are used to patch arteries, and arteries are completely replaced in what is called a bypass operation. Almost 600,000 bypass operations have taken place in the United States since 1975. Along with this increase in surgery on the heart has come an ever increasing interest in the development of a totally artificial heart replacement.

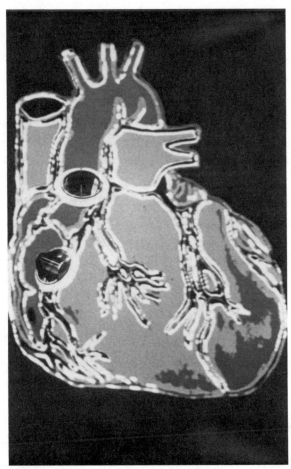

Artificial mechanical heart valves shown in place in the heart.

A partial artificial heart, the heart pacemaker, has helped millions of people whose hearts do not beat strongly enough to lead normal lives. The *pacemaker* is a device that is surgically implanted in the patient's chest and delivers electrical shocks to the heart to maintain regular heartbeats. Available since the 1950s, the pacemaker has been constantly improved, especially in its source of electrical power. Early pacemaker batteries were not always reliable, but today longer-powered nuclear or lithium-iodide batteries are used. Cardiac pacemakers that are programmable are also being made today. That is, the pacemaker's electrical signals can be speeded up or slowed down by radio signal from outside the body.

Other examples of partial artificial hearts are the implantable defibrillator and ventricular assist devices. The artificial defibrillator is a device somewhat like a pacemaker. However, the defibrillator delivers electric shocks to the heart only when it develops a very irregular beat. Ventricular assist devices are for temporary help only. Such a device can be a balloon placed in a chamber of the heart to expand and contract the heart and thus help pump blood. Or it can be

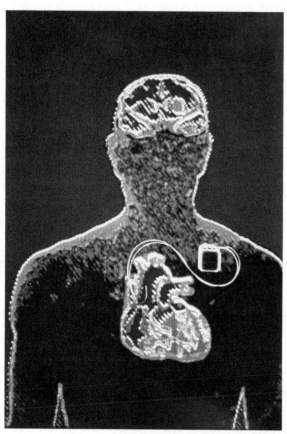

A programmable pacemaker.

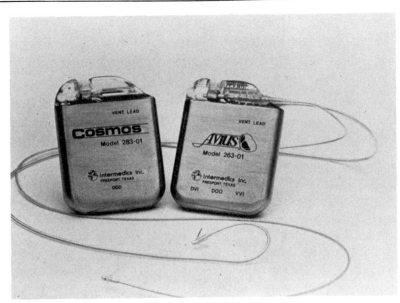
An implantable cardiac pacing system.

a tube inserted into a chamber of the heart and connected to an external pump that assists the heart in pumping blood in and out.

An artificial heart has to be a remarkable invention to replace the human heart. The human heart is both hardworking and durable. It beats over 100,000 times every twenty-four hours, or some three billion times over a person's lifetime, pumping some five million liters of blood during that time. The human heart is powerful enough to keep the blood moving through a person's *sixty-thousand-mile* circulatory system, yet so gentle that it moves the blood without destroying fragile cells. The artificial heart has to be able to do all of these things, yet be small enough to fit in the space of the removed natural heart. And the artificial heart must have a completely fail-safe power source to drive it.

One of the early pioneers in the development of an artificial heart is Dr. Willem Kolff, the same Dr. Kolff who invented the first successful artificial kidney. Dr. Kolff is now director of the Division of Artificial Organs at the University of Utah, where research is being carried out on a variety of artificial parts for humans. Dr. Kolff and his associates have experimented since 1957 with an artificial heart.

Early experiments with artificial hearts were conducted with dogs. Dr. Kolff, who was in Cleveland in 1957, implanted the first artificial heart. The dog survived for an hour and a half. Today, calves have survived over nine months with an artificial heart. The

Five calves, all with artificial hearts implanted in their chests after removal

major reason they have not survived longer is that the calves outgrow the heart. The heart is designed for humans and is not large enough to sustain the blood flow for a calf weighing over three hundred pounds.

of their natural hearts.

Only four times have artificial hearts been used on living humans. In 1969 and 1981, the artificial hearts were implanted by Dr. Denton Cooley, surgeon of the Texas Heart Institute. Both times the artificial heart was implanted because a human donor heart was not available at the time, and the patient would have died anyway. The first patient lived almost three days on the artificial heart before a suitable donor heart was found to replace the artificial one. He was the only person ever to have three different hearts, but he died from overwhelming infections some eight days later.

There has been much controversy over the implantation of artificial hearts. The tremendous costs involved, the feeling that heart transplants offer a better solution, and the use of human beings for experiments are some of the causes of the controversy. Therefore, the federal government's Food and Drug Administration has established guidelines for doing the implant. The surgery can be done only for certain kinds of patients and only by special surgeons. Patients are given very detailed information on how their lives are going to be affected after the surgery. They are going to have to be connected to external machines for life support and live the rest of their lives in a hospital or under very confining conditions at home.

One of Dr. Kolff's co-workers, Dr. Robert Jarvik, has spent a good part of his career developing an artificial heart. This newest creation is called the Jarvik-7.

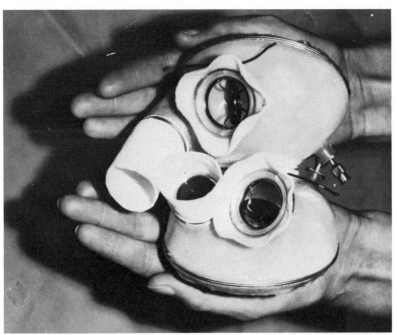
The Jarvik III artificial heart used in early experiments with animals.

Although there are several other artificial hearts being developed around the world, the Jarvik-7 is the most well known since it was the first permanent artificial heart, the one implanted in Barney Clark.

The Jarvik-7 is made of aluminum, polyurethane plastic, polycarbon, and rubber. Like the human heart, it has two inlets and two outlets with valves to keep the blood moving in the proper directions. But the Jarvik-7 has only two major chambers rather than the four the human heart has. The Jarvik-7 fits into the space the human heart takes in the body and is powered by compressed air from sources outside of the body. The compressed air expands rubber *diaphragms*—elastic partitions—in each chamber. The diaphragms are contracted when the air supply stops momentarily. Tubes must be placed into the patient's chest to connect the Jarvik-7 to the outside power sources. The outside power source consists of motors, air compressors, and batteries about the size of a small television set. Placed on a cart, it would allow the person with the artificial heart to move around a little.

In 1984, Dr. William De Vries performed the second implantation of an artificial heart. The patient was William Schroeder, and he received an improved version of the Jarvik–7. Mr. Schroeder was also the first person to use an experimental lightweight portable pump to power his heart, enabling him to move around more easily.

At one time, Dr. Jarvik and his colleagues proposed an artificial heart that would be powered by nuclear

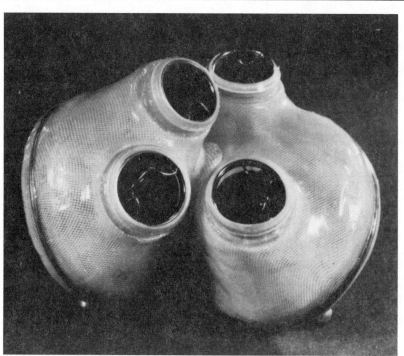
The Jarvik-7 type of artificial heart, powered by compressed air.

energy. However, the project caused a great deal of controversy. Many people were not convinced that it would be safe to have people with nuclear devices in their bodies among the general public. Some felt that they would receive radiation poisoning from nuclear-powered artificial hearts that broke down or mal-functioned.

Dr. Jarvik says, "In about five to ten years, we expect to have an artificial, electrically-driven heart that keeps a patient alive for as long as ten years."

Artificial Lungs

One of the most remarkable artificial parts is the artificial lung. Experimental artificial lungs have been implanted in animals for a few hours, and plans are ready to implant an artificial lung into a sheep.

Like the artificial heart, the development of an implantable artificial lung is a great challenge. The human lung is a very complex organ. Made up of two sacs containing spongy tissue and thousands of feet of blood vessels, the lung has to exchange the blood's waste carbon dioxide for fresh oxygen. Every four minutes, twenty-five trillion red blood cells pass through the lung to supply the body with life-giving oxygen.

The implantable artificial lung operates on the same principle as the external lung machine that has been in use for the past few years. As the blood passes through the lung machine, a membrane of a thin, pliable sheet removes the carbon dioxide on one side and puts oxygen into the blood on the other.

The machine was originally much too large to implant in a human chest, so it had to be reduced in size. This has been accomplished by using Teflon tubing coiled into a plastic bag and connected to the circulatory system. The blood passes through the coiled tubes and exchanges carbon dioxide for oxygen through the walls of the tubes.

This artificial lung is not so powerful as the human lung and is not meant as a replacement but as a helper. Also, three problems remain to be solved. The artificial lung cannot expel fluid like the normal lung, although a tube in the chest wall could drain it if needed. Another problem is that, like all artificial organs, the artificial lung can cause clotting of blood. Clots moving in the bloodstream can be fatal if they clog passages. Patients receiving an artificial lung will have to take medicine to reduce the clotting of the blood, and this medicine can cause hemorrhage. The third problem is whether or not the body will accept the artificial lung. Much more research needs to be done to solve these problems.

Artificial Eyes, Ears, and Other Parts

Most of us are familiar with certain artificial devices to aid the eye or ear to function better—eyeglasses, contact lenses, and hearing aids. And let's not forget artificial teeth—the better to bite with.

Artificial Eyes

Surgeons are using implanted artificial lenses and artificial or transplanted corneas to restore or improve an individual's eyesight. Japanese scientists have developed synthetic fluid to replace the fluid of the eyeball that is lost in disease or accidents. The most

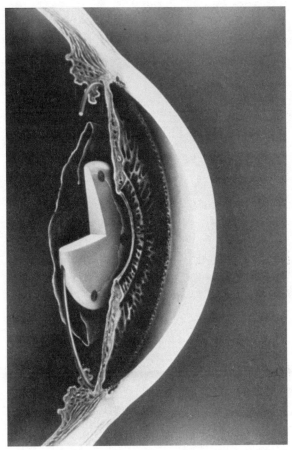

Side view of an implantable artificial lens.

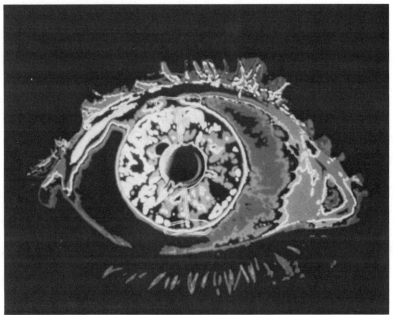

Front view of an artificial lens replacing the eye's natural crystalline lens.

remarkable research is being carried out to help the blind see again through the use of implants in the brain. Sixty-four electrodes are implanted in the portion of the brain that stimulates the area that controls vision. The electrodes are connected by thin wires to a carbon post screwed into the side of the skull. Wires from the carbon post are then connected to a computer. The computer then sends signals that stimulate the

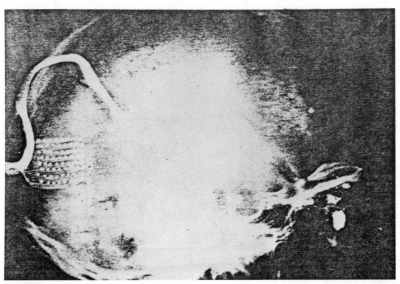

An X-ray of a patient's skull with the electrodes for the artificial eye in place.

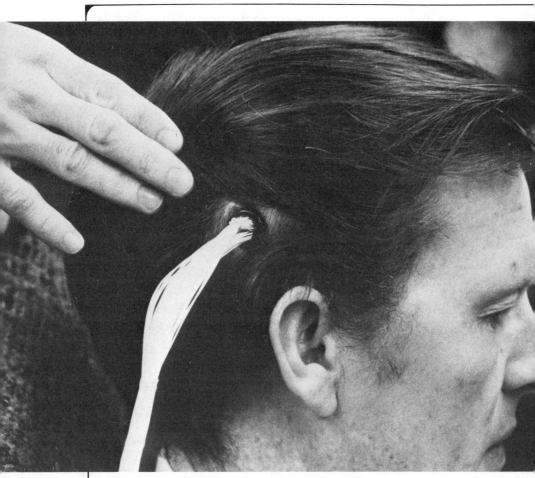

Wires going to the electrodes permanently implanted in the brain of a blind patient.

implanted electrodes in the visual part of the brain, which in turn cause the blind patient to see tiny dots of white light. When the electrodes and the computer are connected to a television camera and the camera is focused on a line on a blackboard, the blind patient can visualize in the brain whether the line is horizontal or vertical. Hundreds of electrodes rather than the present sixty-four are planned for future implants. This amount would allow the patient to visualize pictures.

Artificial Ears

Even though there are a variety of hearing aids available today for the partially deaf, some people have not been aided by them. Certain kinds of surgery have helped others, but for many, nothing has helped. Recently, however, inner ear implant surgery has become available to help these difficult cases.

Surgeons implant a tiny electrode in the inner ear (cochlea) of the patient. The electrode is attached by a thin wire to a battery-powered microphone outside of the body, much like a regular hearing aid. The microphone then carries the sound to the electrode implanted in the inner ear. The electrode changes sound to electrical energy and transmits it to the brain over the auditory (hearing) nerve, which then tells the brain the sound that is being transmitted.

Because scientists lack exact knowledge of how the auditory nerve really works, the implantation of the electrodes in the inner ear is somewhat experimental. For example, placement of the electrode, and also the amount of electrical stimulation to it, is critical to the kinds of sounds that can be heard.

It also must be understood that inner ear transplants do not allow patients to regain all of their hearing loss. What it does do is allow the patients to be able to tell the difference between medium and loud sounds. But the implant gives off an artificial, robot-like sound, so patients must undergo training to understand it.

Scientists are sure that continued research will soon allow them to understand more about how the ear nerves work, allowing them to perfect these kinds of transplants. Some scientists have been experimenting

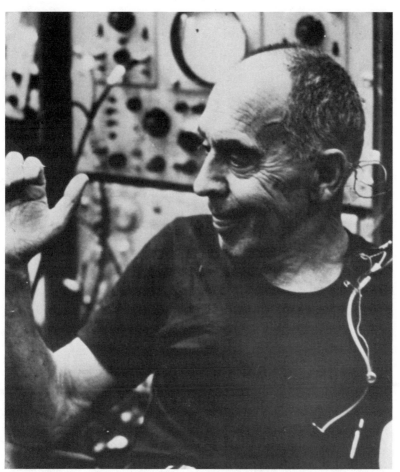

A deaf patient with an artificial ear.

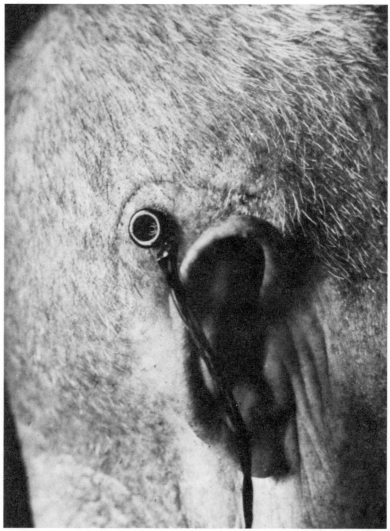

A close-up of the patient showing permanent implant in the skull for the artificial ear.

on replacing the tiny bones around the ear with glass-like parts that transmit sound better than spongy bones, which absorb sounds.

Artificial Teeth

You may remember the story of George Washington and his artificial or false teeth made of wood. We've come a long way from wood, but false teeth still seem to be uncomfortable to put in. Today, two areas of research on artificial teeth seem to be very promising. One is the use of newer materials for false teeth or implants. Some of these newer teeth are made from alumina ceramic, a substance very much like sapphires or rubies. The other area is that of using electrical stimulation on teeth, gums, and bones to stimulate growth or movement.

A Pennsylvania firm is now marketing a device which will allow individuals wearing braces to straighten their teeth in far less time. The battery-powered device is about the size of a dime. At bedtime it is placed in the mouth, and two short wires are placed next to the gums. Painless electric current is given off by the device and causes the bony sockets that hold the teeth in place to move, helping strengthen the teeth. This treatment is said to cut the wearing of braces in half and is thought to be helpful in treating gum diseases, cleft palate, and giving relief of pain to people who wear false teeth.

Fluid Control

Artificial valves to control fluid in the body have been used for some time. One long-time use has been the placement of plastic valves or shunting devices on *hydrocephalic* children, children with accumulation of fluid around the brain. Babies born with hydrocephalus must have the fluid drained from their heads to prevent their being killed by the pressure. But often brain damage already has occurred.

New testing techniques can determine when an unborn child has hydrocephalus. Researchers theorized that if they could remove the fluid before the baby was born, the child would stand a better chance of being normal. Using *ultra-sound imaging*—sound waves to tell position and shape—surgeons were able to place a valve in an unborn baby's head by operating through the abdomen of the pregnant mother. The baby was born three months later, normal, and without a sign of the surgery.

Skin Patches

An artificial device that most of us will be using sooner or later is that of skin patches used to deliver medicines into the body. These devices look like bandages and pump the medicine through the skin directly to the bloodstream so dosages can be delivered over a much longer period of time than by other methods. By bypassing the stomach, dosages can be better controlled, because nausea and vomiting can be avoided and larger doses can be given.

A Device for the Spinal Cord

The *spinal cord* is a bundle of nerves passing from the brain through the *spinal column*—spine—to all parts of your body. When the spinal column is fractured or displaced, the spinal cord can be pinched or cut. Cutting of the spinal cord causes paralysis. The higher in the spinal column the cord is cut, the greater the paralysis, starting with the legs and going up to the arms.

Dr. William Dobbelle of the New York Institute for Artificial Organs has discovered how electrical patterns or messages are sent from the brain through the spinal cord to move muscles. This is the first step to finding a way to send messages by way of electronics and computers around injured portions of the spinal cord.

Pinching of the spinal cord can also cause permanent damage if the blood supply to the cord is cut off. To stop the swelling that causes pinching, a heat exchanger is fitted over the damaged spinal area. The heat exchanger is a small, thin, hollow plastic device with an inlet and outlet through which cold water and alcohol

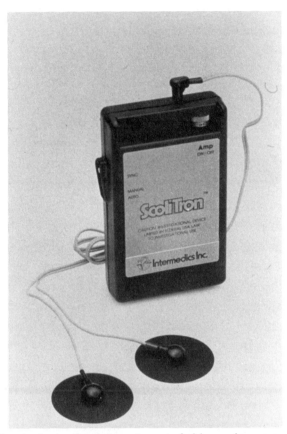

A Scolitron, the first electronic device for the treatment of sidewards curvature of the spine—scoliosis. Scoliosis, which is a birth defect or result of disease, often requires bracing or surgery. The use of Scolitron may avoid these more drastic procedures.

circulate. The surgeon opens the damaged area of the spine, places the heat exchanger on the area, cools it to stop the swelling, and is then able to repair the damaged area.

The Artificial Brain

Scientists know less about the brain than about any other organ of the body. A great deal of research has been done, but the brain, the organ that controls how we think and act, is extremely complex.

Specific areas of the brain are responsible for various functions. However, other parts of the brain can sometimes take over these duties, sometimes by training. One area of brain research is the mapping of these areas and their possible substitutes. Researchers are also investigating the use of electrical stimulation of the brain to try to control certain diseases. Still another important research area is that of transplanting brain cells from healthy brain tissue to damaged tissue to see if healthy cells will take over the functions of the damaged ones. Damaged brain cells do not *regenerate*—rebuild themselves—like cells of the skin and other parts of the body.

In 1981, researchers implanted brain cells from normal rats to those suffering from diabetes. In many cases the rats were cured of the disease. In the same year other researchers grafted healthy brain tissue into rats' brains suffering from Parkinson's Disease, a disease that causes uncontrollable shaking. The rats receiving grafts stopped shaking.

Someday, human beings may be able to duplicate the brain artificially. Artificial intelligence is the name given to the study of the thinking process and how computers can be made to do this. By the year 2000, some scientists believe computers may be able to imitate the actions of the human brain. Already computers can learn by experience, ask questions, write poetry and music, and can even talk. Some day an artificial brain — probably a small, extremely powerful computer—could be placed into a human skull to replace a damaged or diseased brain.

📎 The Future

Bionics is a field that has brought together various professionals—medical doctors, engineers, chemists, physicists, computer and electronic specialists, and technicians. From these individuals and research groups have come the artificial heart and kidney, newer and better artificial limbs, and a variety of other devices to keep humans from dying or to make them better able to live a more useful life.

By now you may be able to see that the "Bionic Woman" or "Six Million Dollar Man" are not so far-fetched. It is possible for human beings who suffer from disease and accident to receive many new body parts. While these parts might not allow the men and women to overturn cars or run sixty miles per hour, they are able to do something more wonderful—they give life. The artificial heart, kidney, or pancreas are truly more significant discoveries than a bionic hand able to tear doors off the hinges.

In the future bionic devices will be highly improved. Devices now tied to outside sources of power will be implanted and have their own power sources. Many artificial parts will rely on electronic sensors or small computers to regulate them. Microelectronic devices will be implanted easily in the body to monitor all sorts of functions. And there will be many new bionic devices.

The future will also see bionics combined with *genetic engineering*—the science of changing or restructuring the unit of inheritance, the *gene*. Through genetic engineering, new parts for human beings may be constructed in the laboratory. Many parts will be combinations of artificial materials and human cells or manufactured cells.

The future is bright for the field of bionics and biomedical engineering. It will take time and a good deal of money to perfect the devices available today and support the inventions to come that will certainly make the quality of life better for millions of people. Perhaps one day you who are reading about artificial parts for humans will be designing, making, and developing them for the benefit of humankind.

Glossary

Biodegradable naturally dissolvable.

Biomaterials those materials used to replace body parts.

Biomechanics engineering of artificial parts.

Biomedical Engineering *see* Bionics.

Bionics engineering of parts to perform human functions.

Cadavers dead bodies.

Collagen protein in connective tissue and bones. Forms scars after injury.

Detoxify remove toxins and other harmful substances from the blood.

Diabetes disease caused by decrease in amount of insulin produced in the pancreas, which in turn causes an increase of sugar in the blood.

Dialysis separating waste urea from blood cells by using a fluid to flush the waste through a membrane that acts as a screen.

Diaphragm elastic partitions (for Jarvik 7).

Femur thigh bone

Fibroblasts blood cells that form tough, fibrous tissue.

Genetic Engineering science of changing or restructuring the unit of inheritance, the gene.

Hemoglobin colored protein (red) blood cells.

Heparin chemical used to thin the blood.

Joints the connecting point of two or more bones.

Ligament thin muscle holding joints and organs in place in the body.

Pacemaker implanted device that delivers electric shocks to the heart to maintain regular heartbeats.

Plasma fluid portion of the blood.

Prosthesis   artificial part. Plural is *prostheses*.

Prosthetics   science of designing and making prostheses.

Rh Factor   a chemical that may or may not be in the blood. Its presence or absence is important in classifying bloods for transfusion. A conflict in Rh factors between mothers and newborn babies can be fatal to the child unless new and compatible blood is transfused.

Scoliosis   sidewards curvature of the spine.

Steroids   chemical compounds in the body that regulate such things as body growth, appetite.

Tendons   tissues that attach muscles to bone.

Ultra-Sound Imaging   sound waves used to tell position and shape of internal organs, growths, fetuses (unborn babies).

Index

53; replacement of, 14, 37, 38. *See Also* named organs.

Pacemaker, heart, 58
Pancreas, 50; artificial, 51, 52, 86
Paré, Ambroise, 15
Parkinson's Disease, 85
Patches, skin. *See* Drugs, delivery systems.
Plastic surgery, 28–30
Pope Innocent VII, 32
Prosthetics, 15, 29, 30. *See Also* named prostheses.

Schroeder, William, 66
Seattle (Washington) Zoo, 19
Silicon chips, 51
Simian ape, 19
"Six Million Dollar Man, The," 11, 86
Skin, functions of, 37; artificial, 14, 37–39
Soviet Union, 34
Spinal cord, 82
Stroke, 36–37

TCP (artificial bone), 25
Teeth, artificial, 15, 20, 30, 70, 79
Tendons, artificial, 25, 27–28
Texas Heart Institute, 63
Transplants, 14, 37–39; 40, 70, 76; of brain cells, 84–85; rejection of, 14, 38, 53; *See Also* Heart, transplants.

United States, 52, 56; Army, 36; Food and Drug Administration, 27, 64
University of New Mexico Medical Center, 51
University of Utah, 17; Division of Artificial Organs at, 61
"Utah Arm," 17–18

Washington, George, 79
World Wars I & II, 16, 19, 42, 45

Yannas, Ioannis, 38

Zyderm, 28–29

About the Author

THOMAS H. METOS is a Professor of Education at Arizona State University with the Department of Educational Administration. A native of Salt Lake City, Utah, he has been both a teacher and administrator in the school system there. Dr. Metos has also taught at the University of Utah and was Curriculum Coordinator for the San Diego County Department of Education. He and his family make their home in Tempe, Arizona.